# NIGHTS UNDER PEACH TREES

Tamron Morris

Cover art by Ciara Kalnbach
Published by Van Rye Publishing, LLC
www.vanryepublishing.com

Library of Congress Control Number: 2020939573
ISBN-13: 978-1-7340344-2-4
ISBN-10: 1-7340344-2-4

# Dedication

To everyone who supported me, thank you.
To Julian and Jaiden, you mean the world to me and more.
To my parents, thank you for everything you've ever done
and continue to do.
To my grandma, Ida Jay, and my brother Kobe.
To my sisters, Jada and Kemeisha.
To all of my friends and family.
Most importantly, thank you to my readers.

# Contents

# Preface

*NIGHTS UNDER PEACH TREES* is a collection of poetry that shines light on heartbreak and how, at times, it might be hard to cope with the feeling of your heart crumbling. But the book also contains poems about the possibility of moving on from heartbreak, finding joy within yourself, and falling in love with yourself. Keeping faith and finding what you believe in are a huge part of this book because they are things that the author had to learn for herself and that she would like to encourage others to learn.

# Introduction

DEAR READER,

This book is for you. No matter who you are, I wrote this book to inspire you, to bring joy to you, and to create a place that allows you to identify.

Regardless of what anyone thinks, I know that you are trying. I know that the demons try to make themselves into your perfect head and implant demented things. But you are beautiful inside and out. And I am proud of you. You have the strength to get out of bed and to continue striving no matter how hard that might be.

Heartbreak and moving on are things I am very familiar with. My heart has been tugged and torn many times, and I feel that I should share those experiences with you through the poems in this book. This book is personal. This is *our* space.

I hope that my words can leave an everlasting impression on you. I hope that you may never have to experience the pain of having your heart broken. I hope you know that you are powerful and you are wonderful. You are simply . . . *you.*

—*Tamron Morris*

# There Is Always a Reason to Smile

THERE IS ALWAYS a reason to smile.
The day is new and refreshing,
The grass is greener,
The sky is a light baby blue.
The flowers are alert, filled with joy,
As blessings are distributed, freely.
Our burdens do not live here, nor can
They leave everlasting impressions
On our character, for there is always
A reason to smile.
Even if we feel empty, depleted, and worried,
We must go on and move as if there are
No anchors to bind our ankles.
The birds circle together in flocks
And sing cheerful songs to a clear sky.
The children run, play, swoop, and bend,
*For these are the reasons we smile.*

# The Power of Believing

THE POWER of believing speaks volumes.
The standard is held high, and there have been
Many nights of perplexed thoughts and
Constant doubting.
"I can't do this," she said,
Scratching her head, her eyes
Marked by exhaustion.
A sigh of relief exits her soft,
Shaped body, and the ability to
Smile becomes harder to accomplish.
All she knows is the ugly side of failure.
In failing, lessons are learned, and that
Is how we grow from within.
Through gritting teeth,
The long, exhausting nights, and tear-stained
Pillows, we are forming into our
Greatest potential. We are stars waiting to
Radiate a blackened sky.
Life became more purposeful when I believed
*In myself when no one else would.*

# If the Stars Could Sing

IF THE STARS could sing,
There would be a great halt, when
Complete silence has taken over.
If the stars could sing,
They would belt out songs of great
Detail, dedicating every last breath to
The weakened, the ill, and
Those who lack faith and mourn for days.
If the stars could sing,
I would ask them to conjure a collection of
Notes that would leave you speechless.
If the stars could sing,
Every peering eye would vow their attention
And consume the intergalactic beauty they
Have stored precisely in front of timid eyes.
If the stars could sing,
They would sing over and over and over,

*And it would never grow old.*

# What Do You Believe In?

WHEN YOU LAY your head to rest,
And you begin to wonder heinous
Thoughts,
Who do you turn to?
When the world grows cold and
Wraps you in its grotesque hands,
What do you do?
When your faith is going down the drain,
And there is no time to save it,
How will you go on?
When the lights are fading at the sound
Of my cracked voice,
Your hands are trembling.
What do you believe in?
When all that is left is nothing,
When all there is
Is nothing.
Where do you go?
Do you pack up and run?
Or do you stay and fight your battles,
    *Like a true warrior*?

# The Sound of Grace

THE WIND howls,
And by now, the atmosphere is
Cold to the touch.
Naked bodies lay flat against
The earth's threshold,
And they weep until they
Can't anymore.
The weight of anguish hangs
Heavily upon their shoulders,
Their backs blotched with cuts, scars,
And burns.
The sound of grace comes roaring,
Bundling every bruised body,
Channeling waves of protection.
Faint, calm whispers strategically find
Their way into her midst.
She is embraced in a calm demeanor.
It was something I hadn't quite seen before,
But she reflected light
And beauty, as I watched her stand firmly
And

> *Unapologetically.*

# The Inability to Cope

MY POCKETS are empty,
With nothing to lend you, but
My heart is full.
I have words to uplift you,
To provide comfort and
Confidence, and to act as branches.
And I am the tree.
Faith sprinkles its way onto your
Sweet tongue,
Replicating the way snow falls.
With each taste, you
Crave the ability to cope in a
Pool filled with misery.
At times, it becomes difficult
To breathe and to be at peace, but
As putrid and as tiresome as it may be,
*There is always room for change.*

# How to Choose Yourself

WHEN THE NIGHT approaches, and
You're wrapped in your favorite blankets
And things, I hope that
It treats you well.
I hope that the constant suffering
Fades away into the dead of night
And that your tears dry completely.
When the morning is here,
I hope that you feel safe wherever you go
And that your life absorbs droplets of kindness.
I hope that you choose yourself
*Now, tomorrow, and in the days and years that follow.*

# Over and Over

OVER AND OVER, my expectations
Are not met, and I cannot help
To imagine a life without the weight
Of guilt sitting on my broad shoulders.
I'd only hoped for clarity
And much given space for additional growth.
It becomes difficult to strive,
And by now, I cannot deal with the
Aching and breaking of these bones.
Over and over, I've dreamt of acceptance—
To be able to live in my truth,
And to
    *Own it.*

# Where Do We Go from Here?

PACK YOUR bags,
Rid your hands of shame,
And wipe your tears.
It is time for a better tomorrow.
The day brings news that trumps
The feeling of defeat.
Where do we go from here?
Go far, far away,
In hopes of never returning to an
Old life filled with old
Friends and habits that don't
Benefit you.
Run away from those who don't
Respect you, the ones who drain too much of your energy,
The ones who fail to understand you.
Expecting too much from someone
Who doesn't grasp the underlying issues of
How you decide to live is
   *A waste of time trying to decipher.*

# The Abyss

SUNKEN INTO an abyss with
Artificial tears,
Disparity rests within my
Bare hands.
I'm shaken.
In my time here, I've outgrown
The need for apologies
But rather absorbed myself in growth.
For, however my life turns,
Whether it be filled with happiness
Or the pain that comes with moving on,
I hoped to be showered in faith,
Coated from my head to my toes.
For I know good things will reveal themselves
To me
    *Soon.*

# It Isn't Worth It

WHEN HE HAS walked away,
Coldheartedly,
It isn't worth pulling yourself apart
In hopes that he'll return.
Hold your head high and your
Shoulders back
   *Because you are the ultimate prize.*

# A Long Road Ahead

THERE IS A LONG road ahead that is dark
And empty but leads the way.
Many are afraid to travel along its
Rough, bricked pavement
And cold, bare atmosphere.
A long road ahead.
It was then, within the dark, when
I figured I was alone. The cool, crisp
Breeze nips at my neck, and
My eyes are squinting.
The burning sensation in my legs spreads
Throughout the rest of my body,
Quickly.
The destination becomes farther with each
Step taken,
But it's coming
    *Soon.*

# The Battlefield

IT SEEMS the closer I come into
Contact with you, the more
It acts as a battlefield.
My cries are as loud as grenades,
Bursting wildly,
And my body is laid flat across
A destructed field,
Slain. Your war cry matches that of
A massive epidemic.
You unfold me like paper,
And when you decide that you've had
Enough, you leave.
I wonder how many times you will do that to me
And when you'll decide to
    *Stop.*

# It's Time to Leave

WHEN YOU no longer become
A priority to him,
   *It's time to leave.*

# The Stars Weep

THE STARS WEEP every single night,
But you cannot see them.
They cry tears made of stardust
And howl to the moon.
Their soft whispers float throughout
The galaxy,
And they feel alone.
Even though they are clusters of light,
They feel dull.
The stars weep when they feel hurt,
Simmering inside of their tiny
Bodies, and they feel useless.
When the sun comes up,
> *That's when their hiding begins.*

# You Deserve More

LET HIM go.
Save your tears and
Your breath over a man who
Does not deserve you.
*Period.*

# Going Away

THERE IS NOTHING wrong with
Walking away from a person
Who does not even know how to
   *Love you.*

# He Wasn't the One

HE WASN'T the one,
And that's alright.
He was a lesson worth being
Learned
  *But nothing else.*

# This Is the Part When We Say Goodbye

IT WAS AT that moment
When all of the resentment I've
Held onto for far too long
Suddenly left my balled fists.
I'm no longer angry—
Rather, tired
Of giving myself to you,
*For you do not deserve a girl like me.*

# Her Name Was Faith

WHEN THERE WAS no one,
There was her.
When the world collapsed,
Bit by bit,
Each crumble, rumble, and shake,
She showed her face.
When there was nothing else to give,
Nothing else to feel,
Her voice sent jolts up my spine.
Her hands wrapped themselves around me and
Kept me warm.
When I ran,
I ran fast enough to dodge my issues.
There she was,
Acting as a blockade.
And when I needed her,
She was there,
        *Each and every time.*

# A Letter to You

DEAR YOU,
I hope that you can learn to smile again.
I hope that you can find happiness within yourself,
Not within him, her, or anyone else.
I hope you live a long life—a life well lived.
I hope that you never have to be trapped in the
Crossfire of love,
And heartbreak, and such.
This letter is for you, and I hope
It lingers with you everywhere you may go.
I hope you learn to trust again.
I hope you learn that it will all take time.
I hope you know that you deserve the world
   *And much more.*

# Sticks and Stones

STICKS and stones
May break my bones,
But I've learned to stop
Believing in you.
My heart is tired.
It has been drained, tampered,
And humiliated.
    *And I just can't do it.*

# The Last Tear Drop

MY SOCKETS resemble droughts
And cannot produce any more tears.
I've yelled to the Almighty.
My fists are held over my head,
With a cloud of revenge in my eyes.
My heart hurts entirely too much,
*And it's entirely your fault.*

# Finding Myself: Part Two

IF I COULD go back in time
And give my younger self a lesson,
I would tell her,
"Choose YOU. In any situation, time,
Or place. Choose yourself and your
Well-being over a man who only
　　*Showers you in lust.*"

# Walking Away

YOU HAVE every right to walk away
From someone who is not treating you
Well. You are too wonderful to be accepting
  *Half-efforts and broken promises.*

# Why Am I So Hard to Love?

SHE ASKED, "Why am I so hard to love?"
It isn't that you are hard to love.
Not everyone is capable of loving you
   *How you want them to.*

# The Good News

WHAT A LIBERATING feeling to

*Find joy within yourself.*

# Paranoia

MY PAST creeps into my bedroom
In the form of dreams,
And they leave me alarmed.
Paranoia gets the best of me at times
And creates an eerie feeling on
The back of my neck.
Twisting and turning,
Back and forth,
   *I cannot shake this feeling.*

# Free

SUNLIGHT PEERS through untouched windowpanes,
And the hummingbirds hum their way into
The free, warm air.
The sound of freedom whistles calmly,
Attracting herds of people,
And I am one of them.
Freedom.
It runs so perfectly off of my tongue,
As my arms are outstretched,
Waiting to embrace every inch of it as is
Possible.
The bells begin to chime,
Filling churches, and cities, and every sidewalk.
It squeezes itself in between the cracks of
My hands and covers me entirely.
When people ask me what freedom feels like,
I say it is a gift and a privilege.
It is something that tastes so delightful,
*And I can finally say that it's mine.*

# Enough Is Enough

ENOUGH IS enough.
I am exhausted from many nights
Of compromising, only to be dealt
A faulty deck of cards.
There are times when your lies
Become bigger than you are, and
*I have no appetite to ingest them.*

# 365

THERE ARE 365 days in a year,
And I have spent them all
Praying for you to find your way back to
Me
   *With open arms.*

# Moving on Isn't Easy

MOVING ON isn't easy,
   *And I'm not sure it ever will be.*

# The Man with No Heart

SAVE YOURSELF the trouble of
Trying to save a man
*Who's unrepairable.*

# Y.O.U.

WHEN YOU OPEN your eyes to
Another day, and the
Sun shines brightly enough
To leave you dazed,
I hope her warmth reminds you of
My skin pressed against yours.
I hope that our song plays on repeat,
Over and over,
Until you grow tired.
I hope you scroll through our old pictures
And that your memory bank goes into overdrive.
I hope that you never have to feel what I did
When you left me
High and dry,
 *Stuck with nothing.*

# Indigo

I'VE DREAMT of lying in a room
With indigo-colored walls
And the silence that surrounds
The silhouette of my body.
All that is left is
You and I.
I let out a sigh of relief.
I feel safe in this space,
Stuffed tightly between these
Indigo-colored walls.
It was like a dream,
With the sound of your voice
Echoing into my ears.
    *I hope the feeling never dies.*

# Torn

IT WAS JUST like that
When the room began to spin,
And once I looked down,
I could spot my heart,
    *Torn into a million shreds.*

# A Selfless Love

I GAVE all that I could,
Willingly,
Selflessly, and without a single
Piece of hesitation.
That happened to be lodged within my
Core.
A selfless love.
Though it hadn't gotten better over time,
There was still a bit of hope that
I saved for you.
I prayed for change,
Although it never found its way to you.
Perhaps it's the way that you
Speak that enchants me all over again.
I've woven through many loopholes,
Trials, and tribulations
And have made peace with coming to dead ends.
With every breath that I take,
I hope that it weakens your knees
And that you realize you were loved,
    *Selflessly.*

# Indestructible

I'M MADE OF a thick layer of
Resilience that lines my body neatly,
And despite what they think,
I am indestructible—
Unable to be
    *broken, cracked, or mishandled.*

# This Thing Called Reality

EACH MORNING,
I make a cup of coffee.
I brush my teeth
And comb my hair.
The day goes by swiftly.
I tap your shoulder,
And you roll over and grin
Ear to ear,
Like no other.
This thing called reality—
Isn't it funny?
When the weight of the world just
Suddenly collapses onto your
Shoulders.
When these small, beige-colored walls
Come closing in,
And I mysteriously float.
Without a doubt in my mind,
I've hoped that you would find your
Way back to me, whether it be at a crossroad
Or in the middle of nowhere.
I pray that your hands find their way up my skin
And around my waist,
Your chin planted into my neck.

This thing called reality is tricky,
And for some reason, I get raveled within its
    *Gnawed fingers that I cannot seem to escape.*

# The Heartbreak Melody

I'VE STUDIED this melody,
Page by page,
And it is the song that I will sing
From beginning to end for a
Lifetime.
I am a mixture of a sad man's song
That drags further along than it's supposed to.
My heart begins to break at the sound of
Your voice, and I become
Swarmed with thoughts of many goodbyes,
And I crack at every single beat that produces
From my chest.
The room spins steadily,
The atmosphere is foggy,
And I cannot deal with the voices that
Fight for a spot inside of my brain—
To completely take over,

 *Leaving me drained.*

# Relax, Breathe, Think

RELAX.
Open your palms,
Shift them facing upward above
Your head, and
Breathe.
Inhale, exhale.
Let the stressors leave your body once
And for all
And think.
Think about what brings you happiness,
And hold on tightly,
Never letting it slip through
Your fingers
*Anymore.*

# Let Him Miss Out

YOU DO NOT have to prove how great
Of a woman you are to him.
Let him miss out.
Your time is valuable and should not be
Spent on a man who cannot appreciate
The wonderful woman you are.
Let him miss out.

    *He's doing you a favor.*

# Don't Take My Kindness for Weakness

DON'T TAKE MY silence for granted
Because you will miss the way that
I once laughed without hesitation.
Don't take my kindness for weakness
Because kindness was all that I've given
To you, tirelessly,
    *And it left me drained and heartbroken.*

# Why?

WHY BOTHER BEING a woman to a man

*Who cannot love you properly?*

# At Peace Again

BY THE TIME the sun is awake
And in full effect,
Her gaze soothes my soft, warm
Skin and I let out a great sigh.
*I'm finally at peace again.*

# Nights under a Peach Tree

MANY NIGHTS have my thoughts wandered
Carelessly, yielding the inflicting pain
That I hold within a bare soul.
For many nights, I wondered why you'd left me,
High and dry, with no
Explanations or goodbyes.
The nights under a peach tree—it's the most
Relaxing spot that I've sat and
Pondered for a while,
And it fills me with joy
    *And serenity.*

# Saving

WHEN IT COMES to saving you or me,
I've chosen to save myself
Because you just aren't worth saving
   *Anymore.*

# A Hopeful Spirit

REMAIN STRONG and hopeful,
*For the bad days won't last long.*

# A Question to My Existence

HOW AM I ABLE to feel again
After so much damage?
There are thorns that once grew
Viciously onto the outskirts
Of my heart, and with
Each movement, there is
A stinging sensation.
My fingertips feel like needles
Pricking away constantly.
To my dismay,
My body feels like it is named
    *Captive to all inevitable things.*

# The Interlude

I'LL LOVE you today,
Tomorrow, and each day
After, but I'm just not sure that my
*Heart can take this anymore.*

# New Beginnings

I HOPE tomorrow brings new beginnings,
A new environment, and
A fresh, clean slate.
I hope you have a chance to feel the
*Happiness you once did.*

# They Never Learn

YOU SHOULD NOT have to teach someone
How to treat you.
You deserve all levels of respect, kindness,
   *And love.*

# Affirmative Thinking

WHEN I WAKE in the morning,
My reflection stares back at me,
And she smiles, profusely.
She is content with herself—
Her curves,
Her hair,
And her slang.
She is the woman that I think everyone
Wished they'd known—
The hardest goodbye
And the easiest hello.
The way her eyes grow big at the
Things that she loves.
Her laugh could fill an entire stadium.
Each step she takes is infused
With the essential elements of
Grace, self-worth, and style.
She is magic.
She is an affirmative thinker,
*From head to toe.*

# The World Is Yours

THE WORLD is yours.
Anywhere you want to go
And anything you want to see,
It belongs to you.
Your happiness revolves around your
Precious head, acting as a halo.
You are so intriguing.
*You take my breath away.*

# Pretty Girl, Pretty Girl, Can't You See?

PRETTY GIRL, pretty girl,
Can't you see?
They are not ready for your
Vicarious boasting.
They are not ready for your positivity
And your elegant strides.
The sway of your bodacious curves
And a firm tone.
They are incapable of accepting everything
That you are,
So own it.
Day in and day out, live a life you
    *Are unafraid of.*

# From Within

MY SCARS represent a garden of
Stories worth being told.
Even far after I am gone, I hope
That I've left my mark
Somehow and someway.
I hope they remember my smile
And the way I laughed, constantly.
I pray to be accepted,
Not by what they thought I was,
But by who I really was.
From within
Was the most beautiful parts that
I've truly expressed, openly.
I am peculiar,
And I own every single part of whom
I've blossomed to be.
  *It is my destiny.*

# Home

HOME WAS once beautiful.
The porcelain glass was my
Favorite, and even though I'm
Older now, I still wish I lived in that
Perfectly bricked house.
The orchids in the backyard were memorable.
I laid my head softly into an oh-so
Beautiful bed of flowers every single day.
When I got older, I found a new home
With you, and I must say,
Our memories that we've created have been swell;
But it is not enough.
Home has never felt like home again.
Your hands are uninviting,
And at times, it feels like I am mixed within
The feeling of leaving you and starting fresh.
Other times, I wish your hands would wrap around me
Like fresh vines around a sturdy tree.
Your kisses felt like thorns rubbing against my skin,
Over and over and over.
For some reason, I enjoyed it.
Maybe it was the thought of someone wanting me?
Maybe things weren't so bad?

>    *Maybe it was just worth giving another try.*

# Timeless

THERE IS a limited amount of time
Left, and I've spent it loving you.
Though timeless,
I'd want nothing more than to spend
My entire life with you,
Dancing across the globe,
Your head resting upon my chest
As we examine the beauty that lives within the stars.
I wish things had gone differently.
I wish I had the chance to go back in time
And love you properly.
I'm on hand and knee, waiting for your
Return, and you haven't found your way back yet.
I'm hoping you will
    *Soon.*

# Fading Away

ALL OF MY feelings were trapped inside
Of an empty bottle,
And they gently rode the waves
Of the widest ocean
   *In hopes of finding their way to you.*

# The Mistaken

WHEN I CLOSE my eyes,
I hope that you will be gone—
Physically, mentally, and emotionally.
I pray that the coldness from the world
Disappears at the snap of my fingers
And that I can finally find security—
Not within you
But within myself.
I hope that after all of this is over,
I still have the chance to love myself
The way that I've begged you to.
I no longer need your sympathy;
I just need to know that I am free from
    *The mistaken.*

# Many Nights Ago

MANY NIGHTS ago,
I wondered if the sparkle in your
Eyes would have grown loud and
Proud, waiting for the warmth
Of my smile.
I wondered if you'd ever grow tired of
My hands wrapped tightly around you.
As I lay my head onto a soft pillow,
I smell your scent.
It is enticing.
At once, I close my eyes until
I am unable to see a thing.
You appear, and my heart smiles until
Her cheeks turn into a pasty,
Tomato red.
The stars shine bright over
A fragile halo.
Many nights ago,
I dreamt of tracing your fingers with
Mine until there was no feeling left.
Even now,
I close my eyes, and I wish to
See the grin that I fell in love with
*Many times before.*

# Breaking Up Is Hard to Do

IT FEELS LIKE I am stuck in a room
That constantly corners me in.
My breathing is cut short.
My hands are losing their sensation
Second by second.
I could not imagine experiencing
Life without you, let alone walking this lonely road
With nothing.
Breaking up is hard to do.
You once were my world,
And there was nothing I wouldn't do for you.
I would give my last if it meant holding you again, gently.
You were the center of my entire existence,
And when you left,
A part of me deteriorated.
The dark shadows opened their arms
And swallowed me whole,
Leaving the room filled with something eerie.
Chills run up my spine,
And the heartache grows rapidly—

*I'm not sure when it all will end.*

# Deep

I'VE FALLEN too deep
Into this thing called love,
And now it becomes harder
To pry myself from its powerful grasp.
It's like my body is submerged in a
Vast body of water,
And I cannot feel anything from my head
To my toes.
The feeling lingers
On and off,
Back and forth, and
All throughout the remainder of my day.
My evening grows cold,
And the subtleness of my emotions quickly
Makes itself known
Onto my bare skin.
I've fallen way too deep
In this thing called love,
*And I am unsure how to escape.*

# Transformation

I'M transforming—
Transitioning out of the aches
That have pricked my narrow fingers for
Too long.
I awaken with my hands faced upward toward the
Sky, and a sigh of relief leaves my body.
Each and every day,
I wondered when life would make sense again.
Regaining my faith,
My belief,
Was the ultimate goal.
I'd unraveled so easily, so gently.
I'm transforming.
I am transitioning into a woman of great faith and
Prosperity.
I am no longer afraid of who accepts me or not;
I've already accepted myself,
And I've accepted every inch that makes me
    *Me.*

# I'd Rather Be Alone

I'D RATHER BE alone than to settle
*For anything less.*

# Leave Him

YOUR HEART is too full.
You are too beautiful.
Leave him,
*And let it be his ultimate loss.*

# My Heart Wants You but Can't Have You

MY HEART mourns from your absence
And prays for your return.
She just wants a glance at those
Dark, brown eyes
That once lit an entire room.
You do not belong to me,
And it pains me to let those words slip
Through the cracks of my teeth.
Vigorous beating occurs.
I want nothing more than every piece of you,
Inside and out.
Your skin tastes like a jar of honey,
Your lips mimic the softness of fresh cotton,
And it feels like I just don't have enough time—
Time to continue loving you for a lifetime.
Each day, I'm determined to turn over a new leaf.
But how can I when you have become distant?
My heart thumps, beats, and flips at the sound of your name,
The gentility in your walk,
And the power you hold in your hands.
It was at this moment that my heart called your name,
From dusk till dawn,
*But you haven't yet replied.*

# Red

THE ROOM'S WALLS are coated in red,
And my yells bounce from ceiling to
Ceiling as the thoughts cave in.
I cannot get you out of my mind,
Even if I try.
It hurts entirely too much
To look you in the eyes after you
Tore my heart from my chest.
Red—
These walls are coated in red.
Out of spite,
Deceit,
And the lies that overspill from your lips,
Over and over.
Through and through,
I've convinced myself this was a love
Worth saving—
A happily ever after, if you will.
It took tons from me, and
Required me to love you more than
Myself.

    *And that just simply isn't okay.*

# Blue Peonies

BLUE PEONIES, blue peonies.
They grow so beautifully.
Their scent kisses the air, softly.
I am amazed at the wonders of the world
And all that it brings.
I am on the road to discovering forgiveness.
I can feel its cold shiver drive up my spine.
When I open my eyes,
I feel the gift of redemption,
Cleansing away at my hands and face.
My heart is full and content.
On my worst days, I catch myself smiling
Ear to ear with the ability
To forgive myself
And to start fresh.
I am better than yesterday,
And I have faith that I will regain the happiness
I desperately long for.
Blue peonies, blue peonies,
You make me feel happy
And strong.
*You were the roadmap back to myself.*

# Raw Emotion

RAW EMOTION is displayed
On my face, perfectly.
The sound of my voice leaves
You shaken,
And my feelings are wound up
Tightly within this
Bottle that sits within reach.
I am afraid to profess my love for you.
I am not sure what to say
Or what you will think,
But I know that my heart resembles
A four-page letter
Addressed to you.
She bleeds ink.
She is boastful,
With plenty to say.
My feelings are true
And raw,
*All the way down to the bone.*

# In Times like These

IN TIMES like these,
I miss the warmth of your lips
Pressed against my skin.
Now that you're away,
Each step that I've taken on this
Earth feels bleak—
Very bleak.
In times like these,
I wish we could smile like we once did
And laugh as if it is only us two that
Make up the planet.
In times like these,
I wish I could come to terms with
Not having you.
In times like these,
I wish I could move on
And forget that we ever existed.
But that would hurt my heart more
Because my heart only wants to know you.
The softness of your voice
And those beautiful eyes.
   *God, this is hard.*

# Inside Thoughts

AM I good enough?
Will I ever be?
Am I a failure?
What do others think?
The many thoughts that roam through
My mind constantly.
Often, I sit with my legs folded,
And my face hangs between my legs.
All I can do is think.
My inside thoughts eat me alive,
And it hurts,
Badly.
They leave me scarred
And sometimes afraid to leave my home.
Their glares sink into my skin,
And they grow like a bad rash.
I'm exhausted.
My inside thoughts get the best of me.
They cloud my head
And my judgment,
 *And I fear that I will lose my battle with them.*

# A Hurt Woman

SHE'S HURTING, but she's strong.
She has more power than
She knows of.
*That is why you must be careful.*

# When They Leave You Out

IT HURTS, I know,
To feel like you are not included.
You *are* wanted.
I've experienced the feeling of being
Alone, and it is not welcoming.
When they leave you out,
I know you want to cry.
I know you want to scream
And throw your hands into the air,
But don't.
You are wanted.
You have people who love you,
People who want you,
And people who need you.
When they leave you out,
Remember these words.
You are not alone.
        *You are surely wanted.*

# Anything

YOU.
Can.
Do.
    *Anything.*

# Paper Hearts

HE RIPPED my heart into shreds
*Like it was made from paper.*

# Self-Love

YOU'VE GOT TO love yourself enough
To walk away from anything that
*Does not bring you peace.*

# Worth the Wait

YOU ARE worth waiting for.
Even if you feel you aren't, you are.
There is a glow in your face
When you speak of the things you love.
You wear charisma well.
I cannot tell you the amount of
Days I have prayed for a love like yours.
I've waited to embrace you
For the rest of my life.
When I look into your eyes,
I see a side of vulnerability that I haven't
Seen before.
It's soft and very subtle.
I'd spend the rest of my life with you,
 *Without hesitation.*

# Gone

I'M SO far gone,
I have no interest in coming
> *Back.*

# Pink Love

LOVE IN MY MIND was the color pink—
Soft, warm, and vibrant.
Love is a part of my vocabulary, and
It rolls off of my tongue, swiftly.
I learned the harsh reality
That love is not perfect.
It has its bumps in the road,
It has ups and downs.
But there was still something magnificent
About it.
Pink love.
Though sometimes love left me black
And blue,
I wanted to hold her hands.
I wished that she would see me,
Clearly,
And accept what I had to offer.
You see, she was a mystery in itself,
And it pains me to think that
There was a small chance of our survival.
Pink love.
Her skin was the warmest place I could
Have been.
Day in and day out,

I've dreamed of awaking to her full face,
With a smile that beamed louder than her words.
I'm in love with her,
But I have to own the fact that she may never love me
Nor need me how I need her.
I am okay.
I type these words with tears in my eyes,
With the sound of sorrow playing
In the background.
This is for my pink love.
I'm not sure when she will get this,
But I hope she does.
I hope the words from this page find their way
Into her delicate hands

*And that she holds them forever.*

# A Part of Myself

A PART OF ME tried forcing
Itself to love you beyond measure,
And when it failed,
It left me shattered like glass,
Coating the floor,
Heavily.
A part of me was left destroyed,
And sadly, I feel at times
It's unrepairable.
My faith runs deep, though.
When I open my eyes in the morning,
I smile harder than I ever have.
I can stretch
And let my feet hit the ground
And feel okay.
Tomorrow brings greater.
 *I know it.*

# Two-Page Letter

I SIT here
Writing a two-page letter
That deeply expresses my
Heartbreak.
With each word,
I feel like my mind whirls
Tirelessly in big circles;
My mind is a puddle of emotions.
I am not sure if I can break down this big wall
That I've taken so long to build.
It blocks you out.
You cannot come in,
No matter how hard I try.
The room is spinning,
And I feel like I am hyperventilating.
Bit by bit,
I just want to scream like there's no tomorrow.
I want to know that I am loved.
I want to be cherished,
But at times I feel like that is too much to ask,
So I stay out of the way.
I can no longer deal with this burning
Feeling within my gut or
The pain I feel in my throat every single day.

I can no longer love you.
You are a contribution to the pain
And all of the guilt that lives in me.
I want you gone.
I want to lose every memory and
Every feeling I've produced for you.
In this two-page letter,
You are the reason I write.
You are the reason I am angry.
You are the reason

*I cannot continue being treated this way.*

# When

WHEN THERE WAS no one,
It was just me—
A lonely soul,
Praying to find its way somewhere,
Someday.
This thing called life can be
Unfair and unusual.
I must not give up, though—
There's so much worth living for.
When I sunk to the bottom of the barrel,
I sat there and thought,
On and off.
There was nowhere or no one to run to
But myself.
It sounds lonely,
But I've learned to enjoy the quiet.
*It allowed me time to learn who I am.*

# Hope Comes by Morning

HOPE awaits me.
She waits calmly for me to take her
Hand, ready to step foot
Into a new, accepting life.
Hope comes by morning,
Ready to embrace me
In her silky arms.
This is new,
And it is different.
 *But I'm glad to be here.*

# When the Trumpets Play

WHEN I FIRST laid eyes on you,
I could hear trumpets,
Loud and clear.
In that moment, I surrendered everything.
You were the one.
My heart beat continuously,
Nonstop, from that day forward.
You are the apple of my eye,
   *My greatest destiny.*

# Heaven-Sent

MY EXPERIENCE with you
Was like heaven on Earth.
It's unfortunate that it came
   *To an abruption.*

# Glorify

HE GLORIFIED my body
Rather than my soul.
He wanted to love my body
More than he could love my smile.
He praised my lips, my hips,
And my thighs.
He wanted one thing,
   *And it wasn't my love.*

# Epiphany

I HAD an epiphany
That you and I would be together
In a new life,
Starting over.
Despite what our differences may be,
I've found a light that lives
Vividly through you.
It reels me in.
    *You are a sight to see.*

# Things Will Get Better

THINGS WILL get better.

*I have faith in you.*

# Sirens

MY FEELINGS go off like sirens,
And it is impossible to contain them.
I feel like I am running down a drain,
Without control.
My mind is over its capacity.
It is hard to tame the hurt that desperately
Tries to make its way through my gritting teeth.
My eardrums are filled with the sound
Of sirens on repeat.
It's agitating.
My feelings leave me wound up
With no place to run—

    *Only into a place of fear.*

# The Sun's Child

IT'S MAGNIFICENT how she shines
And how her presence creates serenity.
There is never a dull moment with her.
She overshadows pain and suffering
And makes a home
Feel like home.
She is everything and everywhere that
*I wish to be.*

# When This Is All Over

WHEN THIS IS all over,
I hope you take the time to heal.
I hope you smile more than you ever have
And pursue the things that bring you joy.
I pray that you experience a happy ending
And that your heart smiles,

> *Forever.*

# You Are Not Alone

MY FRIEND, you are not alone.
You are strong,
Kind,
And capable of anything
And everything that you put your
Mind to.
There is good that lives in your heart.
You are wonderful.
*You are not alone.*

# I Believe in Us

I HAVE FAITH that love will
*Bring us back to where it all began.*

# Come with Me

COME with me.
Love me like you used to.
Hold on to me as if it is the end of
The world.
I don't want to lose you again.
My heart wouldn't be able to handle that amount
Of damage.
Come with me.
Let's do things differently this time.
I don't want to dwell within the things
We cannot change.
Come with me.
Why not?
Your heart is made of gold,
And I've hit the jackpot.
Take my hand,
Close your eyes,
    *And love me again.*

# Fantasy

TO BE WRAPPED within your arms
Is like a fantasy.
I've been waiting for this moment
For a while now,
And I must say, you are
Stunning.
Your presence is refreshing.
You fill my heart with joy.
You are everything that I wished for and
*More.*

# With Love

YOU ARE deserving.
With love,
  *Tamron.*

# From the Publisher

## Thank You from the Publisher

Van Rye Publishing, LLC ("VRP") sincerely thanks you for your interest in and purchase of this book.

If you enjoyed this book or found it useful, VRP hopes you will please consider taking a moment to support the author and get word out to other readers like you by leaving a rating or review of the book at its product page at your favorite online book retailer. For example, at Amazon, you can do so by visiting the book's product page, scrolling down to the section labeled "Review This Product," and clicking on the button labeled "Write a Customer Review."

Thank you!

## Resources from the Publisher

Van Rye Publishing, LLC ("VRP") offers the following resources to writers and to readers.

For *writers* who enjoyed this book or found it useful, please consider having VRP edit, format, or fully publish your own book manuscript. You can find out more and contact the publisher directly by visiting VRP's website at the following web address: www.vanrycpublishing.com.

For *readers* who enjoyed this book or found it useful, please consider signing up to have VRP notify you when books like this one are available at a limited-time discounted price, some as low as $0.99. You can sign up to receive such notifications by visiting the following web address: http://eepurl.com/cERow9.

For *anyone* who enjoyed this book or found it useful, if you have not already done so, VRP hopes you will please again consider leaving a customer rating or review of this book at its product page at your favorite online book retailer. These ratings and reviews are themselves extremely valuable resources for writers and for readers like you.

Thank you again!

# About the Author

TAMRON MORRIS was born in Hinsdale, Illinois. She was raised in a small town, Berkeley, Illinois, by two loving parents, Bruce and Elisha Morris. As a young girl, she began writing short stories in genres including comedy, action, thrillers, and more. While later attending high school at Walther Christian Academy, she furthered her love of writing by taking classes such as American Literature, British Literature, and Creative Writing.

Tamron briefly attended Aurora University as a nursing major, then transferred to the College of DuPage. There, at the age of twenty, she became a mother. Despite the challenges she faced as a young parent, Tamron continued her passion for writing by starting a career as an author. As an emerging voice in the poetry genre, Tamron hopes to inspire women and men to fully love themselves beyond measure.